Discovering Abhimanyu

An anthology of stories on Life
and an everyday person
discovering each other

Parikshit Sinha

Ukiyoto Publishing

All global publishing rights are held by
Ukiyoto Publishing
Published in 2024

Content Copyright © Parikshit Sinha
ISBN 9789362699596

All rights reserved.
No part of this publication may be reproduced, transmitted, or stored in a retrieval system, in any form by any means, electronic, mechanical, photocopying, recording or otherwise, without the prior permission of the publisher.

The moral rights of the author have been asserted.

This is a work of fiction. Names, characters, businesses, places, events, locales, and incidents are either the products of the author's imagination or used in a fictitious manner. Any resemblance to actual persons, living or dead, or actual events is purely coincidental.

This book is sold subject to the condition that it shall not by way of trade or otherwise, be lent, resold, hired out or otherwise circulated, without the publisher's prior consent, in any form of binding or cover other than that in which it is published.

www.ukiyoto.com

to and join the trance. The light was so precious that it changed into five distinct shades of gold throughout the day before switching off into the darkness again.

For the dragonfly, the shard was his hope. It was something different to look forward to every day. He tried flying up and up towards the source of the light each day, a few meters each day. When within the light his tiny little self would burst onto a bright shade of red, his compound eyes, all 30000 of them soaking in every angle, every warmth from the shard, his wings refracting bright VIBGYOR as he flew like a danseur, twirling and jiving for as long and as high his wings could carry him. It is said that dragonflies can't hear, smell, or vocalize, their rice grain-sized brains do not stuff enough grey cells. But our dragonfly. He was beyond these clinical definitions. Floating into the shard of sunshine, with an undefined sense of peace and feverish high at the same time, a psychedelic kaleidoscope engulfed his entire little being. Every day he flew a few meters higher with the hope that someday he would break out from the dingy well and into what lay beyond the shard.

On one such morning, when the shard of light was an in-between the off-white of clotted milk and the ochre of egg yolk, and our dragonfly was in his trance, trying to make meaning of the white particles that floated in the shard, he felt something sticky, something heavy dragging his wings. If he were a human that would almost be the first sign of a stroke. But dragonflies are mere beings and before some more analysis could happen everything just blacked out. Black. Before his 30000 eyes shut close, all at once for one last time he saw the shard fall like a dart on the ugly face of a green-brown frog and its slimy tongue.

The light was back the next day. Sombre for the one celebrating it was gone. But then suddenly between those endlessly floating white particles, was a red particle, slightly transparent, swirling up and up at a pace of its own. The soul of a dragonfly is a liberated particle. So light and so without baggage that nothing at all could pull him down. He rose higher and higher to a widening shard that first was a beam and then a whole sky full of sunshine. And before he finally became one with those white particles and the white light from beyond, the soul smelled the heady unknown of wild roses blooming by the abandoned well. Juicy, sparkling, spicy and citrusy. The dragonfly was liberated at last.

To everyone whose souls are tied to E/5

The Butterfly

He had a reputation. Among the flowers, the bugs, the spiders, and the air. Everyone assessed him through their lenses but in varying degrees everyone agreed that he scanned the entire garden, whiffed fragrances and pollen but fluttered around, without caring much for going into the depths of the texture of the leaves, the flavour of the pollens or for that matter into the pathological, sorry botanical details of everything that grew, lived, and wafted around him.

Then there was the rumour of some professional threats owing to his camaraderie with the birds. They followed him, and he showed them the way. Often fellow butterflies and bees would complain that he brought unhealthy competition in the market and that insects and birds fed off each other but never into each other. True, our butterfly with his ochre-hued wings spotted with brown filigree work had a reputation of his own.

He knew all of this and was forever amused by how little of the big picture can others think, see, and perceive. From the many compound lenses, he saw the world around him, it was an open canvas, ready to be splashed with colours and stroked with lines and the colours and the lines would themselves metamorphose into patterns and those patterns in turn would breathe a life of their own and turn into ever-evolving kaleidoscope of images. There was no time to keep scratching into things for nothing would last forever. What would last is the journey, the joy of moving through the journey, and before his winged self would be one with the light from beyond, he would want to dance and fly and swirl all that he could.

But then you know, our butterfly was not born a butterfly. He hatched from an egg laid into a leaf from the same tree whose fragrance and nectar he now gorges on without worrying much for the age of the bark or the veins of the leaf. He along with a full colony of siblings, hatching around him into helpless caterpillars. Moving green things who had just been programmed to gnaw away at the same leaf that was their cradle. He survived the process of birthing, not knowing where he came from or what was the road ahead. But as was his genetic programming, he kept gnawing at the leaves and got mighty better than all the caterpillars that colony, that garden ever had. He knew which leaves to chew slowly, nibbling each bit as though that was the best meal he ever had, which leaves to just gulp for their taste was venomous, but they helped him grow and pile on fat. At times, the other bugs in the garden even said he reminded them of the legendary Absolem, sitting on a mushroom, smoking away his sheesha and internalizing the Universe's wisdom. Our man listened to all that, smiled or maybe smirked, and kept building his subject matter expertise on leaves.

Other caterpillars mocked him. Unable to chew and grow even half of what he did they asked him what at all the rationale, for one day they would all go into an intermittent siesta, a coma, and who knows if this memory would remain on the other side.

And then one fine morning, when he had just started with a blade of basil that all of his wriggly body started contracting. He was scared, unable to move and then an induced sleep took over him as the cocoon weaved itself around. Our man went into hibernation, with a nanoparticle of basil still clinging to his mouth. While inside the cocoon he soon gained consciousness, but that was nowhere near to what he knew as waking himself up until then. The little sliver of basil kept nourishing him and the cocoon enriched him. He was able to internalize, think through, and see beyond the obvious. Wisdom of life and light had reached him. In a meditative stage, he could see his past, present, and future all culminating into that moment in the cocoon and this moment splitting itself into a thousand mirrors showing him the view of everything that was, is, and will be.

One fine day, the light from beyond transitioned into sunlight from this world. Our butterfly yawned and stretched his wings. These wings too were new but in his time at the cocoon he had seen this coming, and it did not take him much to just spread his ochre wings wide and fly. Fly to the highest skies, where he could see the world around him, and then dive into the nectar of life. Our butterfly had known that salvation and liberation are never an ultimate end goal, in this life, long or short. It's an everyday every moment process. The caterpillar that chewed on leaves, to the hermit's meditative stage inside the cocoon to this flight of fantasy now…nothing is better than the other, nothing more permanent or temporary than the other. Each is a part of the journey and each has its shelf life. Holding on doesn't make sense, letting go and surrendering to the flight does.

About the Author

Parikshit Sinha

Parikshit is a storyteller, spinning corporate narratives and POVs by the day and beyond that, telling tales through his words and art.

His podcast Gentlemannama tells stories of everyday extraordinary human beings. A keen and curious observer of people since childhood, Parikshit fosters a continued interest in the human race - which is also the inspiration in all his writings. He lives in a quaint river valley town, Maithon Dam with his parents, who until today are the wind beneath his wings.

www.ingramcontent.com/pod-product-compliance
Lightning Source LLC
LaVergne TN
LVHW041642070526
838199LV00053B/3504

Contents

Abhimanyu – the coming together of the beginning	1
The Bubble	9
Morning by the window	12
Daarji's Garden	15
The Scarf	19
Board pins in a cigarette pack!	22
Self-love in the time of validation	25
The Dragonfly	28
The Butterfly	31
About the Author	*35*

Abhimanyu – the coming together of the beginning
The Prelude

Subhadra

Subhadra, Subu sat on the windowsill, her twiddling thumbs crushing the carefully ironed Bengal taant saree's loose end. She'd loved wearing sarees and as a child often admired her mother's silks, georgettes, and chanderis and more recently her elder sister's chiffons.

But this taant, a gift from a recently acquainted woman she'd have to call Ma in a few weeks was suffocating. The starched stiffness of the fabric and the weave grazing Subu's skin. Not quite different from the would-be Ma's words a few minutes ago. She'd come to meet and bless the girl all of 19 whom her 30-plus son had fallen for. With a smirk in her voice and an accent quite different, the elder lady had gloated about past reflected glory and about her magnanimity in accepting this match. Subu was still not sure if this was what she wanted. But it was happening and now perhaps she didn't have a choice but to accept. And who knows, the man paints so well and plays the sarod also. He must be a fine husband. The little girl consoled herself. The taant still grazed but the fabric had softened from the thumb twiddling.

The next few days were in a drugged daze. Rituals, relatives, fanatic last-minute shopping, and her mother's never-ending laundry list of last-moment advisory... Subu kept looking at the wedding trousseau with a mix of growing detachment. There was apprehension but the young girl couldn't put a finger yet. He called at times on the landline. She listened; he spoke; the weight of the cradle aching her wrists. When she wanted to speak, he was done and would end the chat. Days continued.

The final wedding day went grand. Subu's parents were such popular social beings and the in-laws had brought along a full band of guests and everyone seemed to have a fine art attaché. Music, sound, laughter colours, and a lot of humidity filled that day in June 1980.

The next morning. Very early. It had rained washing away most of the rice flower designs that had been intricately done on the floor of Subu's home. A few puddles of grey water in contrast with the colours from the night before. Subu with dry eyes got up and washed her face. She now knew what she had always wanted. Alas! it was too late.

Sabyasachi

Sabyasachi, Shobbo, had woken before the crack of dawn and for a moment tried placing himself. He remembered. The night before he'd wedded a much younger but radiating with wisdom Subhadra. He looked around and found his young bride was already up. Maybe she's up to the morning tea ritual. He half lay in bed and lit up a Benson. Not a brand he smoked regularly but this crate was a sort of wedding gift from a cousin in the merchant navy and Shobbo let the smoke curl while it lasts! Finally, he had someone to call his own. His parents had let him grow up with his grandparents as a young child and by the time a young 20-something Shobbo came back to his parents' home, he found a different world. Siblings and parents who were so affectionate and generous, but they seemed like well-orchestrated play or well-behaved guests to say the least. Not his own!

Shobbo closeted himself in his work, painting, and his sarod. The tune of Ahir Bhairon would flow into Bhairavi and drown the cacophony of the household. And then as if destined he had met Subu, the daughter of a much senior director at the company Shobbo had joined. She was everything that he aspired to be but somehow couldn't bring himself to it. Her carefree self though made him uncomfortable often.

But now all will be well. They will set up their nest. He will work and she will make his home. He will play Malkauns, and she will be his rajanigandha, the nocturnal bloom. A bell rang somewhere. Shobbo was suddenly pushed out of his rose-tinted daydream. Who would open the door and face the trouble or whatever waiting outside? A reflux of sour acid filled his mouth.

The Beginning

Subhadra

The rain was lashing hard on the asbestos roof creating a cacophony of sounds and noises, which at its least could be anything but not when you are trying to nap a bit. Subhadra, Subbu lay uncomfortably on the nursing home bed staring blankly out of the window and watching the raindrops pick large bubbles of orange rust from the window grills. Her mind was abandoning, her body exhausted and her thoughts listless. Not more than 24 hours ago she became a mother. The feeling was yet sinking in, and the 20-year-old did not quite know what to do with it. She glanced sideways and looked at "IT". Dark skinned, round-nosed, and narrow eyes but plump at its least. She tried looking hard. Did "IT" look like Sabyasachi, the father, or like her, the mother? None she concluded. The day-old "thing" suddenly started shifting in the cot. At first, she did not notice. 20-year-olds are not equipped to notice when bundles of "IT" start their mobility into the mortal world! Then it cried, first a cat's purr and then a low howl. Subbu, scared, tried to hurriedly look for her mother who was around until lunch time. But oh, she'd left a bit back, to avoid getting caught in the rain. The lazy attendant they were paying was nowhere to be found. Since when have paid attendants not done their duty of sleeping well and dozing the best?

Sighting no one and with the "IT" howling louder and

kicking its little mitten-clad fists in vain hopelessness, Subbu had no choice but to pick up the baby. She held the baby close to her heart, more to hold the tiny little thing closer to her chest and ensure she does not drop "IT".

But the "IT", the boy, had figured out something more precious and throbbing near its mother's chest. Her heart. The same anxious heart that would bind them together in a primal bond. That same heart that would make them have each other's backs when the world would be against them. That same heart that Subbu, decades later would transform into a part of her son's soul, while leaving her mortal body. At that moment, the rains still lashing on the asbestos roof, creating a pitter-patter of sounds and noises, witnessed a mother and son bond.

Subhadra's firstborn; Abhimanyu was nestled in the warmth of his mother's embrace; his safety net. Their journey began.

Sabyasachi

Today, Sabyasachi, Shobbo skipped going to work. Called it a sick leave and that's that. His son, his first one was born last evening. He had grandly named the boy Abhimanyu. After all, Sabyasachi, and Subhadra's firstborn if not Abhimanyu, could be neither. He had looked at his young wife for approval, but she was half dazed with exhaustion and the rest with medication. That's ok, she will not disapprove, he was sure. He had not dared to hold the little one though. Once done with the routine congratulatory messages he had hurried out of the nursing home ward to the nearest post office. A telegram ought to be sent home. His parents anyways were coming the day after, but the first news was a first news. As Shobbo walked to the post office, he could not help but think that the boy neither had his mother's raw gold complexion nor his father's looks. Kind of a bundle in a funny way. But ok, God's graces and we will see.

Back at home the next afternoon, the day of his intentional "sick leave" Shobbo lay in bed and tried thinking of a poem to write for his son. Every year on the boy's birthday a poem written by his father would be gifted. After all what better gift for a man than to reflect on the compendium of poems his father would have written for him every year? In an hour or so, Shobbo had a full scape page full of neatly written lines and he got ready. He will go to the nursing home and whisper the poem in his son's ears. Stuff whispered to babies in the early months stays with them even when their cognitive memory has not evolved much. Or so did the new father think? Could Shobbo ever imagine now, that those poems would be perhaps the bond the two men would form even when they would disagree on the rest of everything under the Sun? No, destiny and future are mysteries and nature has created them thus!

The journey to the hospital though was far from comfortable for Shobbo. Puddles of water, humidity, and an irritating rain. Would it have been better for the rain to stop and then leave? Who knows! Shobbo often wondered, why on earth such elements of discomfort were thrust onto him when others had their ways much easier.

As the young man, by then his enthusiasm for narrating the poem to the newborn diminishing, reached the nursing home ward, he witnessed his son nestled near his young wife's heart, sleeping peacefully.

The moment was magical and Shobbo inched slowly towards the duo, though feeling like an outsider. Very carefully, he placed a finger on the boy's hand just to feel its being of living. And as he wanted to pull away, Abhimanyu clutched his father's fingers. It is this holding of hands that will continue for the several decades to come. The two men will be diametrically opposite and most times at loggerheads but that wouldn't take away anything from the relationship. That same hand that Shobbo, decades later would hold the last thing as his soul would transcend into the finer divine.

Sabyasachi's firstborn, Abhimanyu held his father's fingers; his (and either of their) support system. Their journey began.

Oblivious to the young couple, who were not perhaps meant to be but destined to be, and their day-old son, time not standing still, was moving in slow motion, and chuckling to itself. Do these three vulnerable human beings yet know that this bonding is all that they will have many years later and several journeys after? Will they ever know that there will be a point in time when this bonding will be all that will matter in this whole wide world? Will they ever know that this bonding will give them the lifeline to go on when rest else would have ceased to matter? Perhaps not, decided time…let the mystery of life build on.

The Bubble

About four months back, or maybe a little less. Abhimanyu smashed the glass bubble of hallucinated well-being that he had created around himself. The bubble which he had built with great care and dexterity through nearly a decade, not a little short of that. No one would see that it's not glass but a film of chemicals – something that kids create with soap. No one would see what lies inside. But if all that had to happen, the bubble could not have been a transparent one. Abhimanyu had to colour it. Again, with great care, he filled the outer layer, with pomp, with glitter, with perceptions of a happy life, with nonchalance, with insensitivity, with denial. No one would ever get to know a thing.

Everyone did though. Everyone but him. How could he see the obvious? Abhimanyu was busy maintaining the bubble. Feeding it what he possessed materially to start with and eventually his simplicity, his dignity, his integrity. Feeding it his soul.

But then one fine day, Abhimanyu smashed it. Why did he smash it by the way? Why did he choose that moment to do it? The answer still is a mystery. His mother Subhadra pulled him out hard – the only one he could believe after years of abuse at the hand of the other woman who ironically was supposed to be his life partner, his soul mate. Subhadra had been trying to ever since the bubble had started taking a life of its own years back. She had pulled not factoring in her weaknesses and limitations. She had pulled and had continued to pull. She was not willing to let me sink into the bubble. But of all her pulls why did the one four months back matter as much, one cannot say.

How did Abhimanyu feel about smashing his own Frankenstein? A cold splash hit first and then it burnt hard. Harder than acid corrodes. Harder than the hardest he had ever known. It burnt through everything that he had started believing and living to be true, it burnt through the toenail and right up to the last strand of salt and pepper hair on his scalp. The busted bubble was oozing words, smirks, actions, accusations, and assassinations. Some may heal with time, but a few most definitely materially impair lives forever. Oh sorry! One correction. One should not refer to the bursting of the bubble in the past tense. It is in the present tense. Simple imperfect present tense.

But then life has its organic designs. It is capable of growing and re-growing every time the roots are snipped, and every time the shoots are hacked. It may not grow back into a flowering tree but perhaps into a wild vegetation, with a bohemian charm of its own. But it would grow for sure. Abhimanyu's life is growing too. Again, Subhadra would not have any of that overgrown vegetation around. She nurtured Abhimanyu, yet again. She held him close to her heart and soul, just as her 20-year old self had held her firstborn for the first time and felt his little heartbeat against her soul. Subhadra held her son's hand and slowly but firmly taught him to take baby steps. Steps towards a cleaner, sincere, and simple existence. Steps towards a "new normal". Cleaned his wounds and bandaged them with care. Nursed what was bruised and reassembled what was disintegrated.

Then there was Sabyasachi, Abhimanyu's father. The man of a few words, he silently supported his cub and led him back into the world of books, fine music, and everything subtle that money was incapable of ever acquiring and things that his ex-daughter-in-law, the girl whom Sabyasachi thought as much of a daughter had little regard for. Sabyasachi gave Abhimanyu that assurance of his hand. The same hand, which was now aged and shaking, was not too far from the hold of a finger that a 30-year-old Sabyasachi held his firstborn's little fingers for the first time. He had been a passive man throughout his life but somewhere in these trying times, he activated his strong paternal instincts. No one, just no one could do what she did to his cub. Not anymore. Not ever.

That said, Abhimanyu's battle at the end of the day is entirely his own. The teething troubles are far from over. The bubble tries to cloud Abhimanyu's mind sometimes now too and he knows it will for as long as he lives, playing the Jekyll and Hyde game. But yes, now he sees a light on the other side. White, calm, and assuring. It is light for sure. Sorry again! Another correction. Abhimanyu no more refers to the healing process in the past tense. It is in the present continuous tense.

Morning by the window

The monotonous hum of the alarm clock was at once irritating and assuring. Irritating, as it pulled him out of the loose slumber that Abhimanyu had somehow tried to grab in the wee hours. Assuring, as he realized what his closed eyes tolerated in monochrome was just a nightmare. Yet, as he woke up it all started coming back…the pain, the betrayal, the feeling of groping in a vacuum, and most of all the heavy feeling inside his head. Abhimanyu strode towards the window – the only feature in the room that spoke of life (though not within but outside). As he drew aside the drapes, the morning outside the window was no better. It was a sad rainy morning – the rains had just gotten over and instead of the lush green…it was an uncomfortable grey that enveloped everything around.

The morning by the window seemed no good, he decided to turn his attention and go about with the day. An hour later he was munching buttered toast at the dining table…sipping his cup of Earl Grey occasionally. The hour that had passed between then and now had included him considering drawing a curtain on all this and he had nearly downed a handful of tranquilisers. What held him back in those final moments – let's not get into that…The hour also had him crying inconsolably as the shower jet blurred Abhimanyu's vision and the cold water from the taps

Abhimanyu is an everyday man we see around ourselves almo[st] all the time. Neither perfect nor imperfect but somewhere the[re] in between. He has flaws but little attributes in him, flickers [of] thoughts and actions that are unusual, out of the ordinary mak[e] him a little different. He is someone I would call an everyda[y] extraordinary man. Through this anthology of stories, w[e] see how Life forever had Abhimanyu's back. Without being [a] novella, these stories are interconnected for in each we see ho[w] every time he falls short, life gives Abhimanyu a chance to sel[f-] discover and internalize, view things from another perspectiv[e,] reflect, and shift gears. We also see that every time there was [a] moment worth it, life let him shine like a North Star. The la[st] two stories are about a butterfly and a dragonfly. Not direct[ly] related to our protagonist but bringing the same fluid-spirite[d] continuity and a realization of life and Abhimanyu discoverin[g] each other.

Parikshit is a storyteller, spinning corporat[e] narratives and POVs by the day and beyon[d] that, telling tales through his words and art[.]

www.ukiyoto.com

7 USD | 150 INR

mixed so freely with the warmth of his tears.

The crying had made his head lighter, and the resolve to continue with life returned. If this is what he had to call life…then he better, make it look like life. He put himself together – a full workday lay ahead, then a visit to the lawyer's and if need be, to the police station. And yes, somewhere in the middle of all this, he decided to let a few belligerent elements at the workplace hear a firm no.

The day progressed at its usual pace. The only difference was that the hours at work in the company of those few friends who understood passed way too quickly and those minutes at the dingy lawyer's office, trying to build a case seemed hours long. He had grown wary of all this- repeating those moments of her stony silence and his helplessness – again and again.

But still, he counted today as a day of achievement. First, he could tell some people at the workplace that enough was enough. Second, he had made friends at the workplace who were more than colleagues. A bunch of men in his age group – some married, some engaged, while others happily single. It was interesting to get to their takes on life. And after a chat with them by the coffee machine – he felt a little less like an alien on this planet.

When he drove home, his conviction to live life as it should be was stronger. The boundaries of survival that had once been rigidly chalked out by someone else were beginning to erode. This was his life – it ought to be his way. The last time was just to be treated as an ailment and Abhimanyu is now on his journey to recovery.

The next morning again the alarm sounded its usual time. Only now our man woke up with a much fresher taste of life within his soul. A sparkling morning with yellow sunshine greeted him as he pulled the curtains aside. The grey of the sky yesterday is now replaced with an azure autumn. There might still be a few dark clouds here and there…but overall, it was a bright sunny day. A day worth it!

Daarji's Garden

He walked into the large hall, cleansed of its furniture and adornment. The floor, otherwise, too with gleaming tiles looked especially shining clean and draped in carpets. Sticks of white flowers, rajanigandha, jasmine, and magnolia (apparently from Daarji's legendary garden) mixed with sandalwood incense intoxicated the early summer afternoon. Almost towards the farthest corner of the hall, on a white tableclothed pedestal stood Daarji's magnified and framed photograph. His smile was always calm, soothing, and lending an air of assurance. Around him more flowers and incense and beside him someone with a harmonium was softly crooning Hari Om Tat Sat.

Abhimanyu walked up to his grandfather's picture. Stood there looking at the older gent's eyes and quietly placed the wreath at the foot of the giant frame.

Soon the hall filled up with all kinds of people. Immediate and distant family, Daarji's work friends, senior citizen club members, and the extended community of humans who at some point had been touched by the older gent's kindness. Abhimanyu sat quietly and tried listening to the cacophony streaming in from all corners.

The conversations seemed to be not as much for Daarji as they were about him, and more importantly and funnily enough everyone who spoke made their selves a primary character in the anecdote with the older man cast merely in support. Anecdotes of kindness, coincidence, magnanimity, worldly wiseness, etc. Some people also had pathological questions about Daarji's last days. Who met him the last, who saw his morning texts the first...

Abhimanyu sat there quietly, listening to all these conversations, belted out with such eagerness by these visiting mourners. As though narrating these anecdotes over multiple glasses of cool coconut water and lassi was their sole purpose in dispensing a great responsibility towards Daarji's legacy.

Abhimanyu also wondered how large a person can be of his grandfather's stature who when remembered manifests into several distinct personas than a single human being.

And then the last days. For the past several months Abhimanyu kept planning and kept rescheduling his visits to the ailing old man. Sometimes work, sometimes social engagements, and at times sheer exhaustion with life. The visits kept getting postponed. Every time he would call up Daarji, the old man, kind as ever would assure him that he knows how busy a man trapped in the scheming ways of the world could get. Quickly following those conversations, the two men also agreed that they would meet and take a walk around Daarji's garden-the soul nourisher as they often humoured. The old man had started spending a lot of time in the garden lately and had theories on how the flora interacted with him.

Alas, the walk would never happen. Alas, the visits too would no longer be needed. The soul may have lost its chance to be nourished.

Drowned in his thoughts, Abhimanyu hadn't noticed that the remembrance party was over, and the mourners were departing. He followed the trail, quietly but suddenly decided to take a detour towards the garden, housed in the rear of the villa.

The marigolds were still blooming, not yet ready to call it a season, while the Zinia and the Pansy had gradually started revealing their multi-coloured buds. The omni-blooming bougainvillea was resplendent in three vivid colours across the garden walls. The garden perhaps had yet not processed that their nourisher was gone and continued blooming in anticipation of him. Perhaps in a few days, they'd be tired and will start wilting.

Suddenly, a kaleidoscope of butterflies, all yellow with brown patterns on their wings fluttered out of the marigold bushes. It was as though the wait was over. The soul nourisher had returned. Abhimanyu kept following the winged fairies, plucking dry leaves here and wilted buds there.

An hour later, he called Daarji's daughter (a spitting image of her father who unfortunately was trolled enough in the just-concluded remembrance of how she was still in New York and had not flown back). He asked her if he could visit the garden sometimes and soothe his soul.

She laughed heartily with a tinge of grief and said, Abhi, it's a symbiotic relationship. You nourish and take care of the flora and it reciprocates the love. I could never gather the time or the opportunity to tend to it while the original nourisher lasted. But you my boy, carry on the legacy if you can. It's just not a bunch of flowering trees and plants but the thorns and the weeds too which need as much attention. It simply isn't the marigold but the gardener who depends on this garden. If you can own the soul, the heart, and the magnanimity that my father left behind, you will find in return unconditional nourishment. Think about it, the gardener will have the keys for some more time.

Abhimanyu perhaps had his answer.

The Scarf

"Sir, may I help you"?

"Sir"

Abhimanyu was kind of shaken from his listlessness. It dawned upon him that he had been standing at this specific counter admiring a silk scarf since, who knows, he'd lost touch with time.

The State Handicraft emporiums are a treasure trove in themselves. Abhimanyu loved window shopping in these emporiums. As a child this is one hobby, he fondly shared with his mother. But then she was weary of worldly traps as she'd aged and these days Abhimanyu was quite a solitary explorer.

Anyways, this scarf had caught his attention and drifted him into a sea of thoughts the moment he had walked into one of these outlets today. A rich tusser silk with unusual ikkat prints on its borders. As he stood there admiring the scarf, his thoughts sailed to the several such scarves, that he'd been stocking up through these years. He always justified these acquisitions as his love for handicrafts. But somewhere deep down he was in denial. Denial of the fact that he would have loved wearing these. Denial of the fact that he feared that the high-browed upper-middle-class society around him would brand him if they saw him with a scarf. Denial of the fact that he had a right to wear these and look and feel good about himself as much as his friends from across a spectrum, had the right to openly flaunt their lifestyle choices. He supported alternative sexualities and orientations and their struggles with all his soul but then he also felt that straight men too are boxed into a closet and need to come out of it – perhaps with greater force.

The environment in which Abhimanyu was brought up templatized men's dressing choices into black, white, navy, and grey – much like the society templatized the emotions that a man could have. He could either be dominating, caring, protective, affectionate, leading, and in charge of his emotions and those who depended on him. Any show of sensitivity, fluidity, fragile emotions, and an attempt to deviate into shades other than these was often met with stifling discomfort, snide comments, or still worse, stony silence. But then, since Abhimanyu had walked out of his acidic marriage and finally found time to focus on himself, these templates had seemed to matter less. Success was limited though. His parents were extremely supportive where their son's emotions and wellbeing were concerned. But they were of a different generation. Any outward attempt for Abhimanyu to express his fluidity was not something they were quite comfortable with.

Abhimanyu had started questioning all of this. What did he get by adhering to these templates? Zilch. It brought him a lot of professional success and within the extended family, his oratory skills and presence were acknowledged. But somewhere he also knew that it was as though people around him were waiting for him to come out of the closet. And they thought themselves liberal enough to acknowledge that a closet could only be related to one's orientation or gender identity. That the closet was bursting at its seams for an ordinary, yet extraordinary everyday man like Abhimanyu – this was nowhere in the society's dictionary. "Sir, may I help you"? By now, the salesperson's patience had started wearing off and this was the third time he was asking this middle-aged man who seemed quite "normal types" and visited their emporium often. "Yes please, bill me for this scarf, and don't bother packing it. I will wear it right away".

A few minutes later, Abhimanyu stepped out into the fading winter sun, the scarf firmly but daintily draped around his neck and suiting his grey tweed jacket quite much. He felt the mild warmth of the scarf delicately cozying up his neck and giving it the perfect armoury to brave the winter outside. And yes, as he glanced at his reflection in his car window before getting in, Abhimanyu admired how the scarf did not need to stand on its own. The vibrancy of the tusser accentuated by the grey of the tweed. The flamboyancy of the ikkat border balanced with the crispness of his shirt. Abhimanyu smiled at himself.

Life's answers are perhaps these!

Board pins in a cigarette pack!

Spring cleaning. The idea isn't as glamourous as the word but given his OCD, he always liked setting aside a weekend at the end of February each year to fold away the winter wear into neatly tucked bags, re-arrange the summer wear on the top shelves, air the wardrobe and empty the drawers. The drawers in themselves were treasure troves. One dedicated for the neckties and suspenders, one for the accessories and scarves, and one for knick-knacks and this and that. This story unfolds when Abhimanyu had just finished with the rest of the room meticulously and had started with the this and that drawer.

Something grazed his fingers lightly as he was emptying the drawer. He pulled out the little devil from under a stack of UNO cards. A crimson red pack of Dunhill, the brand name embossed in gold, and the proud maker's name, British American Tobacco, engraved in a watermark on the sides. No, this pack did not carry any cigarettes. Instead, it had a handful of rusted, grown black with age board pins. The sort that one uses to pin up things on a soft board.

He kept looking at the pack for a while, trying to remember how it landed there in the first place. More amusingly of all things why was it stuffed with board pins? And almost suddenly he could close his eyes and smell a mixture of eau-de-cologne and tobacco. The smell belonged to a distant uncle arriving in his parents' household some 2 decades back. The uncle had earned a certain fortune outside the homelands and his visit was a celebration. To our man's childhood memory, this was nothing he had previously experienced and all he had wished for at that point was some personal attention from the just-returned uncle.

Soon though he had been bestowed some personal attention. In the form of the uncle volunteering to look at his evening lessons for the duration of the stay. Starting with a fair share of novelty and mystery of something entirely new, the sheen had worn off too soon. The uncle was a taskmaster, and he was a meek child. There were lessons every morning and evening, particularly in mathematics. Nothing was ever enough to please the uncle though, who would keep smoking the Dunhills as he discoursed his excellence at the subject and demeaned the child then man now citing mediocrity. After every such lesson, he would be graded, and the uncle would pin the test sheets on the soft board atop his desk with board pins. To the child then and to the man now, it had not made much meaning. All this strict way of parenting, all this shaming and ridiculing. Did they think it led to a better outcome?

It was just an episode lasting about 2 weeks in our man's entire life of 40 years, and when it ended, our man had carefully packed the board pins in an empty Dunhill pack and kept it with him. At that point, he had just preserved those board pins. No rhyme or reason and eventually they ended up in the this and that drawer.

By now he was awakened from his slumber and instead of the eau de cologne, all he could smell was a combination of dust, stale tobacco, and rusting iron. He thought for a moment and emptied the rusting board pins into the dustbin, flattened out the pack of Dunhill with care, kept it back in the drawer, and got back to spring cleaning.

Self-love in the time of validation

The first few sentences were all that mattered. Once he could get that out of his way rest of it seemed like a cakewalk. As though someone invisible had already created the storyboard and the cause-effect relationships in his head. Abhimanyu just had to fill in the blanks. Character arcs emerged on their own and took charge of themselves in his writings. An hour or two of solid battle with the keyboard and he would cook up something that started getting likes, reposted, and forwarded nearly as soon as he posted them across his social networks. A dedicated group of followers comprising social butterflies, swag-infused youngsters, swashbuckling influencers, and a vast pool of everyday people. They read him up, commented, trolled, and did everything consciously or otherwise to help drive traffic on his Instagram and blogs, numbers on X, and comments on Facebook.

There was a certain pressure to keep belting fiction week after week, but he enjoyed the adrenaline rush. Deadlines, expectations, project planning, eye for detail, and enriching content were here too but somehow this gave him a far higher, far psychedelic high than the sterile environment of the office screens. That was one part of his Before, he did not quite wish he visited.

Today, headwinds had stuck from the moment go. The random power outages meant that he had to make do with writing on the smaller laptop screen, while the larger monitor was shedding its load. Add to those random domestic sounds that distracted him. Well, there were days when the household gossip and cacophony were part of his creative process but not today. Then there was the subject itself. He had started writing on self-love. His character was hell-bent on becoming semi-autobiographical as much as he tried weaning it away. Surreptitiously, the invisible storyboard maker had infused little anecdotes, experiences, and realizations from his own life into the character that he found hard to take them off.

Okay. So, this was his last attempt. Else he was ditching the whole idea. What would happen at the most? The website and app traffic would be down. He would compensate for some of that with posts on his morning tea and evening walks.

He began writing afresh, surrendering unintentionally to the devices of the storyboard and the character. Words started piling on, constructing themselves into sentences and paragraphs. Those in turn became voices and emotions. Emotions about his self-love. That love that had stayed bundled and crumpled inside him for ages. That love that he was so sensitive to not show to the frivolous world of hashtags outside. He wrote, his character evolved, and his eyes swelled.

That first unrequited love in college, the second heartbreak in adulthood, and the catharsis when he was

40. He wrote it all. Every instance, every moment. As he wrote, so many raw nerve endings got their closure, some balmed into comfort, some coultered out. At the end of the exercise, the lump in his throat that had built up through this writing process had eased out.

He leaned back on his chair, threw his head into the air, and, humoured. After all these years of writing, creating fictional characters, and manipulating them into yielding in a way that would make his literature look fancy and paperback elitist, what was today? A puny character, his creation could bring all this and after all this time.

He typed the last sentences, setting his character free of all guilt and pent-up emotions, and took a little bio break. Hoping to splash some cold water and put together his thoughts on how to position this best within his social media handles. After some time, he was back at his desk. He decided not to publish this. His first thought was to just delete it. Instead, he fired a printout to read at leisure at night. His social media followers woke up the next day to a single-line post.

"Seek love and not validation. The rest my friends is all incidental!"

The Dragonfly

In a forest, not so long ago, maybe it still does, there was an abandoned well. Somebody someday had dug it up but now all it had was a green sludge of slime-infused water, breeding with aimless, effortless mosquitoes, and a huge colony of frogs. The frogs and the mosquitoes lived life on a loop. Devouring on the slime and each other and pooping things out. Their thoughts were assembly line driven, confirming the infinite slime and blood in, poop out the loop. Nothing more, nothing less. They bred eggs, tadpoles, and all, stayed in the well, and at some point, obliterated in the eternal stink.

Quite mundane eh! If I were you, I would stop reading this right now and smell something nice or think something good.

Speaking of good, within the well-lived dragonfly. Let's not get into how he or the egg that he came from got there but he was perhaps Jonathan Livingstone Seagull in another life. For he was the only one that noticed or rather I should say everyone knew but he was the only one to notice that oblique shard of sunlight that came through the mouth of the well, several feet higher up. A round ray of gold, where infinite molecules of white dust danced as if fairies in a trance. The ray of hope, the golden lining which lit up everything it fell on. The shard brought with itself a fragrance so heady, so wild that it would make anyone leave whatever they were up